Tales in Rhyme

Beauty and the Beast

Sia Gupta

Om KIDZ
An imprint of Om Books International

Beauty and the Beast

I will tell you a tale in rhyme.
That once upon a time,
There was a girl who avidly read
Books everywhere, even in bed.

She lived with her father, all alone.
On her face, her beauty shone.
One man actually came to her pleading
'Marry me! and please stop this reading!'

This girl named Beauty, refused.
The man was totally confused.
He looked smart; his name was Hunce.
But to say the least, he was a dunce.

One day, Beauty's father said
About a science fair he had read.
He was going to showcase his invention
At the great global science convention.

He wanted to win as much as he could,
But for that, he had to go through the woods.
So he bade farewell and said good bye,
And on his horse, he trotted by.

Into the woods so very deep,
The dark forest gave him a creep.
Then suddenly, some wolves attacked,
The power to fight them, he lacked.

Through all the trouble and the hassle,
Beauty's father saw a huge castle.
He somehow created a distraction,
And then put his plan to quick action.

He ran through the castle gate,
No longer could he just sit and wait.
He went inside, shutting the massive door;
There were more surprises for him in store.

A grand chandelier above his head,
A warm and cosy, inviting bed;
A sumptuous meal laid on the table,
He quickly put his horse in the stable.

He licked his lips looking at the meal,
His mouth watering, he could feel.
To just look, he couldn't anymore bear,
So he sat and ate on the big, grand chair.

At first, cleaning his hands off the dirt,
He ate his meal in peace and comfort.
He, then, moved around to see more,
The grand castle, he began to explore.

But after what he saw next, he sincerely prayed,
For there was a beast that made him afraid.
The Beast growled and said, 'Why are you here?
You are not welcome, I am making it clear.'

'But as you have dared to enter,
You man, so soft and tender.
You will stay here for eternity,
And will never return to your city!

Beauty's father couldn't convince the Beast;
So while the Beast was having a feast,
He sat and worried about his little girl,
So delicate and sweet, charming as a pearl.

Beauty now, was worrying even more.
Her father was in trouble, she was sure.
It had been a week, way too long.
Something was definitely very wrong!

Beauty climbed on to her horse in haste,
Her riding course, at last, wouldn't go waste.
Then on the magnificent horse she rode away,
Hoping every second and praying all the way.

She had to find her beloved father so wise,
She could almost hear his woeful cries.
In the jungle she saw the palace of the Beast;
She ventured inside, not afraid in the least.

In the hall, the only thing in sight
Was a teapot, with a spout on its right.
Beauty fiddled with it and it said,
'Hey, can't you see I'm going to bed?'

The teapot turned around in a slow crawl;
Beauty was shocked and said nothing at all.
'It's a girl!' it said in stunned surprise.
'Oh my dear, I just didn't realise!'

All the other things she took note,
Began to rise as well as float.
They were all completely shocked.
The candle flamed while the rocking chair rocked.

The mantle-piece then began to shake.
Beauty wondered if she was really awake.
Finally, the clock said, 'Who are you?'
'I am Beauty, How do you do?'

'And why on earth would you be here,
Forgotten your way, have you my dear?'
Said the teapot, recovering from her fright,
And looking quite merry and bright.

'I'm here to find my father who is lost.
I have to find him here at any cost.
Please can I take a look around?
I promise I won't even make a sound.'

'Well if you do insist, you might,
Just don't go to the tower on the right.
And change your dress, have a meal,
After this, much better, you'll surely feel.'

'Oh! so kind of you,' Beauty said with relief.
Presently she looked ragged, was her belief.
She required food for her growing appetite;
It had been a long journey through the night.

Beauty had her meal first,
She also quenched her thirst.
From the wardrobe, she wore a dress,
The outfit would surely impress!

Beauty began her search instantly.
The things never let her feel lonely.
She searched almost everywhere,
Except the Beast's private lair.

She searched the dungeon to see,
Her father was there tied, not free.
'Oh dear father!' Beauty softly cried.
To escape, her father must have tried.

'I will set you free right away
And we can be on our way.'
Before Beauty could be of assistance,
She heard a noise in the distance.

Suddenly, a mighty beast came in.
On his face, there was no grin.
'What are you doing here?' he wondered;
This question to Beauty, he thundered.

Beauty said without any fear,
'To take my father, I am here.'
The Beast then angrily made his firm demand,
'Leave! and never come back!' was his command.

Beauty whimpered and began to cry.
To save her beloved father she did try.
'Please may I be exchanged with my dad?
Please allow it or in worry, I will go mad.'

The Beast took a moment to think,
While Beauty's heart began to sink.
Then he said, 'Fine! that I will allow.'
And he left without a wave or a bow.

Beauty's father was then sent,
Into the woods away he went.
Beauty was now on her own,
She was starting to feel alone.

Suddenly the clock, candle and teacup came.
'Don't cry, you are stuck here, it's a shame.
The master is truly not so bad, you know;
Into a steady friendship you may even grow.'

'If you don't like him, we are still here,
So in this castle, do not have any fear.'
Beauty managed to give a weak smile,
And asked, 'Where will I stay meanwhile?'

'The tower on the left should do,'
Said the candlestick and his crew.
Exhausted, Beauty went with the clock,
It marched tick-tock, tick-tock, tick-tock.

Candlestick and teacup excitedly went to the Beast,
While he ate a platter of meat and bread made of yeast.
And they said, this could be your only chance,
Just go ahead and ask the lady for a dance.

She may fall in love with you,
And break the curse for us too,
For many-many years back,
Was a prince, kindness he did lack.

He was throwing a fancy ball;
And telling lies, big and tall.
When they were disturbed by an old dame,
Into the luxurious castle hall she came.

She asked, 'Oh! please may I stay?
Just for this night and one more day?'
But the prince just smirked with an evil grin,
While the dame tried to keep up her chin.

He yelled across to make her get out,
He forbade her with a loud shout.
Suddenly, the lady changed herself,
She was now a fairy with ears like an elf.

She turned the prince into a beast, a devil,
Making him look ugly and really evil.
As for the other people and their kids,
Now they were pots and pans with lids.

She magically produced a beautiful rose,
With all the petals stuck together, close.
The fairy, in the end, said her final word,
Which she hoped everybody heard.

She said the petals would fall and scatter,
And for all there that would be a great matter.
'Before all the full-bloomed petals shall go,
An act of true love, someone must show.'

'Otherwise, the prince will be a beast for ever,
Be transformed to a human, he would never.'
That brings us back to this very day,
Where the candlestick had his final say!

'To her, dear, you must be nice and kind,
I'll come to you everyday and remind.'
The Beast just ignored him and shook his head,
While Beauty, to one of the best rooms, was led.

As she entered, she marvelled at the grace,
There was surprise on her glowing face.
Beauty said, 'What a wonderful room!'
It nearly took away all her gloom.

There was a large and soft bed,
And dresses; yellow, white and red.
Alas! Even after a good night's sleep,
Beauty still wanted to wail and weep.

But the candle took her to the library,
There were books of every kind, even history.
Over there, the Beast sat with a book,
Not even a glance at Beauty, he took.

Beauty just gazed at everything,
In a soulful voice, she began to sing.
The Beast then turned around,
And said, staring at the ground.

'Would you, my lady, like to see
This world of books with me?'
Beauty smiled shyly and said,
'Any of these books, have you read?'

'Oh, Yes!' replied the Beast, 'I love to read;
You can also take all the books you need.'
And so the friendship had begun,
The Beast was actually having fun!

Beauty was happy but a little sad,
She was really missing her dad.
The Beast noticed, gifting her a mirror,
It had a magical, sparkly shimmer.

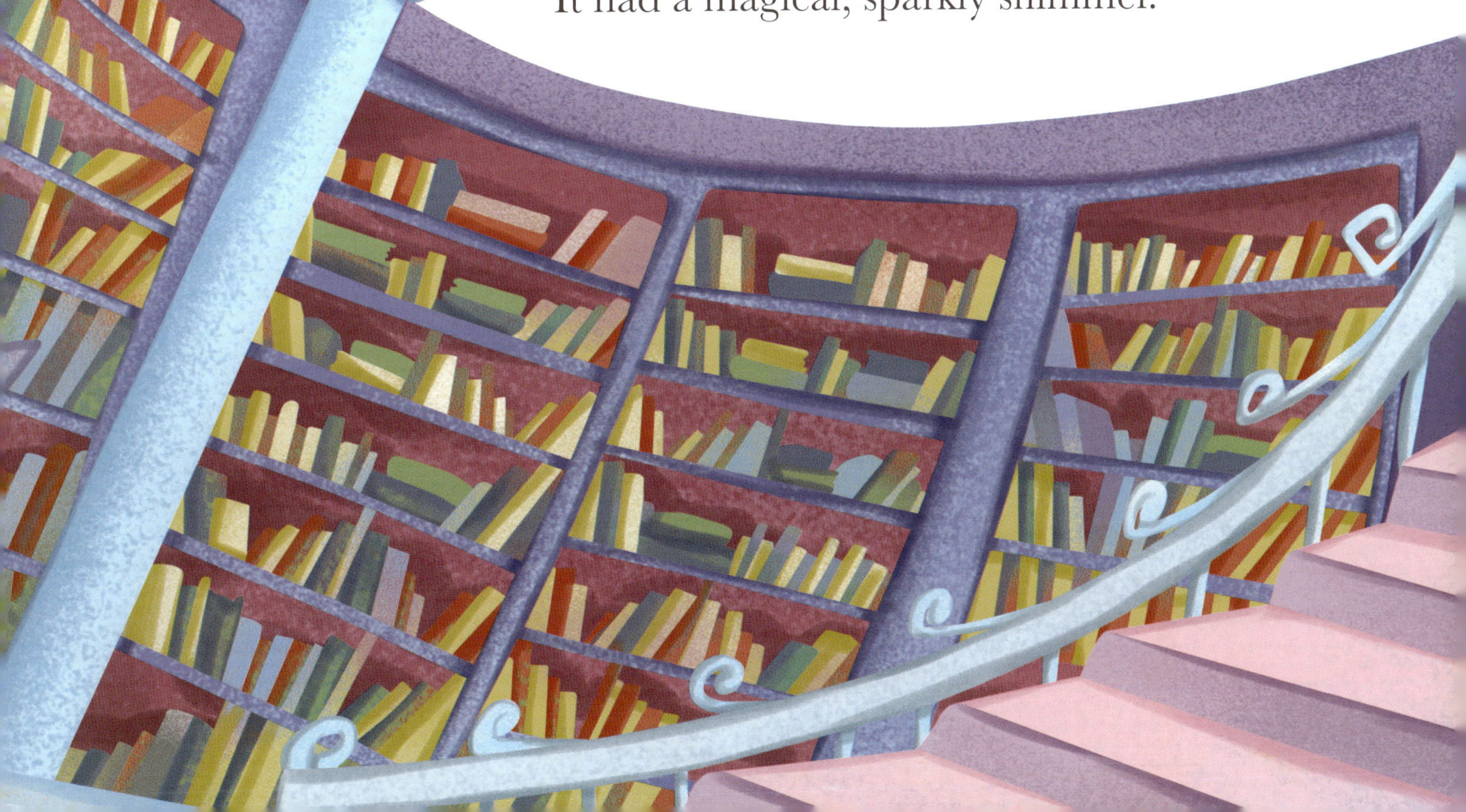

From that mirror, Beauty could see
Her father, who was her only family.
For the Beast, she started to care,
He was actually gentle, kind and fair.

The Beast started growing in her affections,
She was still not allowed in his private sections.
Meanwhile, her father reached his home town,
He had promised to bring the mighty Beast down.

He told the villagers to rescue his daughter,
And together the Beast they would slaughter.
Hunce and the other angry villagers agreed,
And towards the castle, they started to proceed.

They reached the castle and stormed the wall,
And started breaking things in the grand hall.
The Beast heard and went to protect Beauty,
For he now knew and felt that it was his duty.

They attacked the Beast, all at once.
Beauty yelled, 'Oh stop, stupid Hunce!
Don't harm the Beast.' Beauty said
To Hunce, who wanted him dead.

But Beauty, in their rage, the mob did ignore.
The Beast lay like he was dead on the floor.
'Go away! You killed my wonderful friend,
Who I will always love till the very end.'

With these words, she broke the spell,
Just as the last petal of the rose fell.
The Beast transformed into his old self,
A handsome prince, if I say so myself!

The things also did transform,
They regained their human form.
Beauty watched in a state of shock,
Suddenly dressed in a pretty frock.

The prince then humbly asked her for marriage
While standing in front of a royal carriage.
Her eternal love, Beauty did truly confess.
She even kissed him eagerly and said, 'Yes.'

The villagers realised how sweet the Beast was,
They were sorry for the trouble they did cause.
Beauty and the Beast married in joy and laughter,
And they lived happily ever after!